The Malted Falcon

Bruce Hale

HARCOURT, INC.

Orlando • Austin • New York • San Diego • Toronto • London

www.HarcourtBooks.com

Library of Congress Cataloging-in-Publication Data
Hale, Bruce.
The malted falcon: from the tattered casebook
of Chet Gecko, private eye/by Bruce Hale.
p. cm.
"A Chet Gecko Mystery."
Summary: Chet Gecko and his partner Natalie
try to find a missing valentine and the
winning ticket to a fantastic dessert.
[1. Geckos—Fiction. 2. Animals—Fiction.
3. Schools—Fiction. 4. Valentines—Fiction.
5. Desserts—Fiction. 6. Humorous stories.
7. Mystery and detective stories.]
I. Title. II. Series: Hale, Bruce. Chet Gecko mystery.
PZ7.H1295Mal 2003
[Fic]—dc21 2002011593
ISBN 0-15-216706-4

Text set in Bembo
Display type set in Elroy
Designed by Ivan Holmes

First edition
A C E G H F D B

Printed in the United States of America

To my cool cousins, the Gibbs kids

A private message from the private eye . . .

I love a mystery—any kind of mystery. Like, if the plural of tooth is *teeth,* why isn't the plural of booth *beeth*? If ignorance is bliss, why aren't more folks happy? And, if you can pick your friends and you can pick your nose, why *can't* you pick your friend's nose?

Naturally, you'd expect an appetite for mystery in a private eye. That's me—Chet Gecko, finest lizard detective at Emerson Hicky Elementary. (Of course, that's just my opinion, but it's one I value very highly.)

The only thing I like (almost) as much as mysteries is sweets. Millipede marshmallow bars, fungus-weevil milk shakes, and vanilla Earwig Supreme send me every time. My idea of a balanced diet is a cookie in each hand.

So you'd think that a case involving sweet treats would make me as happy as a dung beetle in dinosaur poop. But you'd be wrong.

When the ooey-gooey hand of Fate dropped this one case in my lap, it was all I could do to stomach it. My investigation revealed that not all dames are made of sugar and spice and everything nice. And that, given the right motivation, some kids are capable of anything.

But in the end, I didn't let it put me off my appetite. After all, whoever said you can't have your case and eat it, too, never met Chet Gecko.

1

Fire Drilled

When my morning began with a lumpy bully, a fire drill, a mysterious stranger, and a cootie attack—all by recess—I knew it would be one of those days. A day when you wish you'd strangled your alarm clock. A day when you wish you'd perfected that fake cough and stayed home sick.

Unless you're a detective, that is. We eat trouble for breakfast, with a side order of danger, hold the mayo.

The whole thing started with the *plop* of a pop quiz onto my desk.

Mr. Ratnose's quizzes are scarier than a broccoli-and-liverwurst smoothie. Especially when you haven't done the homework.

I stared at the sheet. The questions made about as much sense as training wheels on a *Tyrannosaurus rex*. Cold sweat trickled down my cheek.

Only one thing could save me. . . .

Ring-ah, ring-ah, ring-ah!

The fire bell.

A smile curled my lips. Saved by the drill.

Mr. Ratnose's pointy kisser wore a puzzled frown, but he gave us our marching orders.

"Single file, everyone," he said. "Line up."

We formed a line and trooped out the door. Just my luck, Shirley Chameleon cut right in front of me.

"Oh, hi, Chet," she said, as we walked down the hall.

"Shirley."

She had big green peepers and a long, curled tail. If I went for dames, I might have thought she was pretty cute.

But this gecko doesn't go for dames.

"It's . . . um, would you . . . er," Shirley mumbled.

"Spit it out, sister," I said.

She turned a delicate pink. "Would you be my valentine?" asked Shirley.

"Absolutely."

"Really?" she said.

"Yup," I said. "When monkeys fly out of my nostrils."

Shirley's face fell like a kindergartner's home-baked cake. "Chet Gecko, you are so mean!" She rushed off, taking her cooties with her.

I sighed.

Just ahead of me, Bitty Chu, a goody-good gopher, turned in place. She gave me a dirty look.

I gave her a dirtier one. She turned back around. What makes dames so ding-y around Valentine's Day?

By this time, we had reached the playground. Lines of kids covered the grass like army-ant sauce on a sundae. Natalie's class stood by ours, but my mockingbird pal was out of earshot.

Teachers huddled at the front of the line, swapping complaints. We weren't going anywhere, so I checked out Natalie's class.

Like my own, it was packed with mugs, mopes, and misfits. I recognized Wyatt Burp, a bullfrog who could belch like an opera star, and Paige Turner, a spoiled titmouse in a cashmere sweater.

Paige waved at Bitty Chu. They stepped across the gap between the lines and began whispering. All I caught was something about a "moldy falcon."

Secrets fascinate me. I drifted toward the gossiping pair. Then I bumped into what felt like a tree trunk.

"Hey!" said the tree. I glanced up. A tall, spiky reptile with enough peaks on his back for a small mountain range was glaring down at me.

UN

"I'm allergic to hay," I said. "Can we make it clover?" (Not one of my best quips, but why waste the good stuff on a stranger?)

"You bumped me, mate," he rumbled. "Apologize."

"All right. Sorry you got in my way."

The lumpy-looking mug snarled. "Wise guy, eh?"

I smirked. "Not really. I'm a C-plus student."

"I oughta teach you a lesson," he said, clenching his fists. The big guy eyeballed Paige and Bitty, who'd turned to watch.

"Fine." I put my hands on my hips. "You can start by teaching me what kind of wacko reptile you are."

The creature's eyes narrowed. The spikes on his head got spikier.

"What dipstick doesn't know a *tuatara* when he sees one?" he said.

I drew myself up. "The kind who's never seen a *too-ra-loo-ra* before, that's who. Dipstick yourself."

We stood toe-to-toe, locked in a sneer-a-thon.

Soft wing tips brushed my arm. "Chet?"

It was my partner, Natalie Attired. A mockingbird with impeccable fashion sense, she was sharper than a vice principal's tongue. Just then, she wore a worried frown across her beak.

When she tugged, I stepped back.

"Ah, you've met our exchange student," she said. "Little Gino, Chet Gecko."

The tuatara bared his teeth. "And he'll be flat gecko if he keeps buggin' me."

Before I could make a snappy comeback, the school bell rang *all clear.*

"Come along, class," called Mr. Ratnose. "Let's move out."

I nodded at Little Gino.

"Next time, mate," he said with a sneer.

"Promise?" I asked.

As I turned to march back to the room, I reflected. *It's a good thing I don't have much to do with Natalie's class,* I thought. *You couldn't pay me to hang out with those weirdos.*

But just like the kid who took a pop quiz blindfolded, little did I know how wrong I was.

2

Croak-and-Dagger

After the morning's excitement, recess was as welcome as a Pillbug Crunch bar in a bag of celery sticks. I made tracks for the playground.

The swings were swamped, and Natalie was elsewhere, so I settled for a game of catch with Bo Newt.

We fell into an easy rhythm: toss, run after the ball; toss, catch; toss, run after the ball. I was fetching one of Bo's wilder throws from the krangleberry trees, when something went . . .

"Pssst!"

"Really, Bo!" I said. "Beans for breakfast?"

"What?" called my salamander buddy.

Hmm. He hadn't made the sound.

"Pssst!"

I looked down at the ball. Could a softball spring a leak?

"Hey," came a whisper. "Over here."

Oh. Behind a bush, a shadowy figure lurked.

I stepped closer.

"Close enough," it whispered.

Peering through the branches, I could just make out a frog in a floppy hat and sunglasses.

"Okay," I said. "Why the *pssst*?"

"I need to talk," the frog whispered.

"So talk."

"With you. Alone."

I glanced over my shoulder. Bo was waiting. I

checked out the stranger, who had sounded suspiciously like a girl.

"Come on, Chet," said Bo. "What's the holdup?"

"How do I know this isn't some kind of Valentine's trick?" I asked the frog.

It shifted impatiently. "You don't. But I want to hire you."

I hesitated.

"For double your usual fee," said the amphibian.

I picked up the ball and tossed it to Bo. For double my fee, I'd risk the cooties.

"See ya later," I said to my pal. "Duty calls."

As I plunged into the bushes, Bo shouted, "Hey, Chet. If you gotta do your duty, why not use the bathroom?"

The frog led me to the prickly heart of the thicket. Thorns scratched my legs. Branches slapped my face. The smell of overripe krangleberries—a cross between grandma's perfume and wet doggie odor—filled my nose.

At last, Secret Frog and I crouched face-to-face.

"Why all the croak-and-dagger stuff?" I asked.

The frog tugged the hat lower on her head (and it *was* a her). She briefly lowered her shades. Her eyes shone large and luminous.

"I'm in danger," she said huskily. "If a certain someone saw me talking to you, I—I don't know what would happen."

"What kind of trouble are you in?"

The frog's webbed foot grabbed a branch for support. "Sister trouble."

"What?"

"Maybe I should explain," she said.

"Naw. I love talking in circles."

She offered a shy smile. "I'm Dot," she said. "Dot Maytricks."

"Chet Gecko," I said. "But you knew that."

"Chet, my sister is the one with the problem."

Seemed to me, Dot had a problem, too: getting to the point.

"And her problem is . . . ?" I asked.

Dot's wide mouth drew tight. "It's embarrassing," she said.

"So are my math grades, but you don't see me crying." I shifted my feet for comfort. "Look, I graduate in a couple of years. Are you gonna spill, or what?"

The frog looked down, took a quick breath, and spilled her guts.

"My sister, Courtney, is in love."

Yuck. I *knew* this case had something to do with cooties.

"Bully for her," I said.

"The problem is," said Dot, "she's in love with the wrong kind of guy."

"What, a teacher?"

She shook her head. "Worse. A roughneck."

I took a shot in the dark. "And you're sweet on the same roughneck? Hey, I'm not Dear Scabby. I don't do love advice."

Her lower lip trembled. "Please," she said. "I'm not in love with him. Courtney gave him a valentine and I want it back."

"For the chocolate?"

"No, to save her reputation."

My legs were starting to cramp from crouching. Any more of this, and I'd walk like a duck the rest of my life.

"Did you ask him nicely?" I said.

"Pretty please with sugar on top," she said.

"And?"

"No luck."

I tried to straighten and bonked into a branch.

"What do you—*ow!*—want me to do, get it back?"

"Would you?" she said. Dot rested her hand on my arm. "I'm sure if someone strong like you tells him to, he'll give it up."

I plucked her hand off. "It's worth a try," I said. "Who's the mug?"

"A fifth grader. Bert Umber."

"Sounds like a colorful character."

"You could say that."

"I just did. Slip me four quarters, sister, and Chet Gecko is on the case!"

Dot rummaged in her bag. She dropped the silver into my palm. Then she gave me the lowdown on Bert Umber—his habits, his haunts, and his weaknesses (which were few).

"Now, can we leave these bushes before I start sprouting berries?" I said.

She held up a webbed hand. "Wait!"

"What?"

"We can't leave together; Bert might see."

I nodded. "Good thinking. I'll go first."

"Chet!" said Dot. "I thought you were a gentlelizard."

"Who told you *that*?"

She lowered her shades enough to bat her big reddish peepers at me.

"All right, all right," I said. "Froggies first."

Dot crept through the bushes. I waited a bit, then followed.

By the time I stepped out of the greenery, Natalie was waiting. "Hey, Chet," she said. "Here's a joke for you: How do crazy people go through the forest?"

I looked at her. Nothing short of burning tail feathers could stop Natalie from delivering her punch line. I shrugged.

"They take the psycho path!" she squawked.

I rolled my eyes and brushed leaves from my coat.

"So, what's with all the bushwhacking?" she asked. "You beating the bushes for clients?"

"Sure," I said. "Just leaf it to me."

She winced. "Wood you knock it off? Tell me: Any luck?"

I couldn't think of any more shrubbery puns, so I jingled the coins in my fist.

"Twice our fee for half the work," I said. I pointed to Dot's retreating figure. "And that's our client."

Natalie watched the frog and frowned. "*Hmm.* She looks sorta familiar."

"You know her?"

"Hard to tell," said Natalie. "All you reptiles look alike to me."

"She's amphibian."

Natalie shook her head. "Amphibian, vegetarian . . . doesn't matter what she eats. I can't tell her from the next green-skinned critter."

I marveled at my mockingbird partner. They say a bird in the hand is worth two in the bush, but they never say what the heck you're gonna *do* with a bird in your hand.

3

Strong-armin' a Marmot

Lunchtime may not come before *detection* in the dictionary, but it does in my book. I put our new case on ice until I'd sampled the cafeteria's delights. (The boll-weevil crumb cake was especially tasty.)

Fed, full, and fit as a fiddle, I dropped the lunch tray on the dirty stack. My hat was stained, my T-shirt was ripe, my coat was rumpled. I was everything the grade-school private eye should be.

And I didn't care who knew it.

Natalie and I were headed for a showdown with Bert Umber.

But first, we needed some backup. You know the old saying: Better to be safe than . . . smooshed by a fifth grader. (Or something like that.)

Tony and Bo Newt were tussling behind the library with a massive badger from the football team. Bo ducked under the badger's swing.

"We're going to talk some sense into a fifth grader," said Natalie. "Want to help?"

Tony tripped the football player, and Bo bounced off the guy's belly like it was a fuzzy trampoline. "Count us in," he said.

According to Dot, Bert Umber usually played basketball at lunch. On the way to the courts, I laid out our strategy.

"Remember," I said. "Don't start anything unless he won't listen to reason."

"Got it," said Tony.

We reached the basketball courts. Sweaty kids crowded the asphalt, throwing elbows, taking wild shots, and shaking up their lunch. Everyone looked bigger than me.

"How do we tell which one's Bert?" asked Natalie.

I turned to a sleepy-looking rabbit lounging on the grass.

"'Scuse me, bub," I said. "Where's Bert Umber?"

"Hah?" he asked. "Burp Dumper?"

"Bert Umber!" I repeated, louder.

"Ya?" a deep voice rumbled behind me. "Who vants him?"

Checking over one shoulder, I found myself eye to eye with a furry elbow. Up, up, up I looked. He was a slick marmot with the usual assortment of muscles under a glossy blond pelt.

Blond isn't a natural color for marmots. I suspected Bert and Lady Clairol were on a first-name basis.

Craning my neck, I looked him in the face. "Chet Gecko . . . and company," I said, jerking my thumb toward Natalie and the Newt Brothers.

"Make it schnappy," said Bert. "Ve're playing ball." He stepped onto the grass.

"Now, Chet?" whispered Bo.

"Not yet," I muttered.

I sized up Bert. With a lug this big, might as well try the easy way first.

"We have a friendly word of advice," I said, "about your choice of girlfriends."

Bert frowned. "You mean Sally or Lili?"

Sally or Lili? No wonder Dot thought he was a bad influence.

"Neither one," said Natalie. "We mean little Miss Maytricks."

"Who is dot?"

"Ah," I said, "you know her sister."

"Whose sister?" said Bert.

I folded my arms. Fine. If he wanted to play dumb, so could Chet Gecko.

"Never mind the acting," I said. "Just give back the valentine you got from Dot's sister."

"Vhich sister?"

"*Dot's* sister," I said.

Bert's forehead wrinkled. "You keep saying dot sister, but you don't say vhich sister."

Tony Newt stepped forward. "Want us to whomp him, Chet?"

I clenched my jaw. "Not . . . yet." Addressing the thick marmot, I said, "Listen, pal. Are you gonna give us Courtney Maytricks's valentine, or are we gonna make you?"

Bert's massive fists landed on his hips. He bent down and snarled. "*Make* me? You und vhat army?"

That did it. "*This* army!" I said, waving the Newt Brothers forward.

"Hi-yeeeeaahhh!" they shouted.

Bo and Tony flew through the air like bargain-hungry moms at a clearance sale. Natalie and I charged forward.

Violence is a private eye's last resort. But it does get a suspect's attention.

"Yaaah!" yelled Bert. He staggered under the impact like a soap opera queen at cancellation time. Bert twisted to and fro, but couldn't shake us.

"Don't pretend you—*unh*—don't know Dot Maytricks and her—*oof*—sister, Courtney," I grunted.

"Who's—*aargh*—pretending?" said Bert, a bonehead to the end.

At last, Natalie hit him behind the knees, and we all went down—*thud!*

A shadow fell across the tangle of private eyes and meatheads.

"Chester Gecko?" rumbled an unmistakable voice.

It's never good news when they call me by my full name.

I squinted up at the foul-tempered fat cat called Principal Zero. We were in for it now.

Our white-furred boss man smiled, fangs twinkling. "Is this your handiwork?"

I nodded.

"Well done," said the massive cat.

Natalie and I exchanged a glance.

Bert said, "But—"

"Someone told me *this* hooligan was responsible for our unexpected fire drill today," said Mr. Zero, pinching one of Bert's ears. "And now he's going to get what's coming to him."

That was principal-speak for *the spanking machine will wail today.*

We climbed off the unlucky marmot. But as I watched him get up, I realized we were no closer to helping Dot.

I tried one last time. "Come on, I know you know Dot Maytricks. Green frog, huge red eyes, wears a floppy hat and shades. She wants her sister's valentine."

Principal Zero grabbed one of Bert's arms and Vice Principal Shrewer the other. As they marched him off, Bert twisted to look back.

"I don't know about ze shades and hat," he said. "But dot sounds like my girlfriend, Lili Padd."

I frowned.

"Und she doesn't have a sister."

Kids parted before Principal Zero and his captive. They rubbernecked as Bert went off to get his. Everyone loves to watch a wreck.

"What do you know?" said Natalie. "I *knew* that frog looked familiar."

"Huh?" I asked.

"Lili Padd is in my class."

My tail twitched. "Class or no class, it's time we had a little talk with the forked-tongued Miss Padd."

"But, Chet, frogs don't have forked tongues."

"This one does," I said.

4

Let Sleeping Frogs Lie

Lunchtime was drawing short—as short as my temper. We had just enough time to grill Dot, or Lili, or whatever her lying little name was, before it ended.

I thanked Tony and Bo Newt for their help, and Natalie and I took off. (Actually, she took off; I had to hoof it.)

While Natalie searched for our client from above, I trotted down the halls with eyeballs peeled. I checked the gym. No frog. The sandbox. No frog.

She was as hard to find as a bully's conscience.

Suddenly, the hall loudspeaker crackled. "Paging Chet Gecko, hotshot private eye. Your fly is undone."

I started to glance down, then stopped. Natalie clung to a nearby branch.

"Ha, ha," I said. "Any fly that gets near me *will* be undone."

"I found her, Chet," she said.

"Lead on, MacBird."

At the edge of the playground, a frog sat on a wall, sulking. Natalie and I arrived. She jumped.

"Okay, sister," I said. "What gives?"

Dot or Lili or whoever tried on an innocent look. "Why, what do you mean?" she asked.

I crossed my arms. "Nobody makes a monkey out of this gecko. Why did you lie to me?"

The frog hung her head and took off her shades. "I was afraid," she said.

"You'll have to do better than that," said Natalie, frowning.

Lili/Dot hopped up and began to pace. I was getting tired of not knowing what to call her.

"Where do I start?" she said.

"With your name," I said. "Lili, right? Not Dot or Daisy or Humpty-Dumpty?"

"It's Lili," she said.

"And you don't have a sister, do you?" asked Natalie.

"Nope."

Natalie raised her eyebrows at me. Progress at last.

"So, why the dodge?" I asked.

Lili fiddled with her sunglasses. "I didn't want word to get around."

"What word?" said Natalie.

"About the love note," said Lili.

"What love note?" I said.

This was like pulling teeth. And frogs don't have teeth.

I rubbed my neck instead of throttling hers and took a deep breath. "Okay. Pretend we have no clue what's going on." (Which was pretty close to the truth.) "Explain it in small words."

Lili looked up, round eyed. "I, um, gave Bert a valentine."

"So?" said Natalie. "Girls do that around Valentine's Day."

"But I changed my mind," said Lili, "when I found out he already has a girlfriend. I want my card back. He won't give it to me."

I scratched my head. "So why all the song and dance about a fake sister?"

The frog turned away. "Kids talk. If they knew about my valentine, I'd be a school joke."

I felt for her. Poor kid.

"You lied to us," said Natalie.

Lili put the shades back on and leaned toward me. "Sorry," she said. "I wanted you to scare Bert. I thought maybe if a big, strong gecko like you shook him up, he'd return it."

Natalie and I exchanged a glance. I'd met some screwy dames in my day, but Lili put the *nit* in *nitwit.*

"Will you still help me?" asked the frog, with a tremor in her voice.

"Give us a minute," I said. I pulled Natalie out of earshot. "What do you think?"

"I think she's flakier than my mom's garden-slug turnovers," said Natalie.

"Still," I said, "she's already paid our retainer."

"Yeah . . ."

"And she does need help."

Natalie snorted. "Sure, mental help."

I couldn't argue with that. The smartest thing would be to drop Lili like a red-hot fire ant. Which is why I said . . .

"Let's give her a second chance."

Natalie batted her eyes. "Whatever you say, you big, strong gecko," she said, in a dead-on impression of our client.

"Don't *you* start."

We walked back to Lili.

"Okay," I said, "we'll help you get the card back."

She grabbed my arm. "Oh, thank you, Chet. Thank you."

I freed myself before the cooties could get under my skin.

"But no lies," said Natalie. "Or else. So, what does the envelope look like?"

"It's pink," said the frog. "And on the outside, it says *Lili + Bert.*"

Yuck. I wouldn't touch a valentine on a bet. Natalie was going to carry this one when we found it.

"If we can get it back, we will," I said.

"Yippee!" cried Lili.

Yippee, indeed. The more I knew about this case, the less I liked it.

Our client had told us more stories than Mother Goose on a midwinter's night. And I sensed that other surprises were in store. But still, I stuck with it.

That's dedication for you. Or dim-wittedness, I forget which.

5

Hiccup or Ship Out

Sometimes, a private eye has to tell a fib or bend the rules to solve a case. That's regrettable. And it's something you can't do well unless you keep in practice.

Fortunately, I practice often.

It was quiet reading time. Mr. Ratnose kept an eye on the class while he graded papers with the other—a trick only a teacher (or a chameleon) can master. Silence covered the room, thicker than the peanut butter in a peanut-butter-and-june-bug sandwich.

Keeping my eyes on my book, I let out a loud *"hic!"*

Mr. Ratnose glanced up. I could feel his gaze.

"Hic, hic!" I covered my mouth and looked around.

"Chet Gecko?" said Mr. Ratnose.

"Yes—*hic*—teacher?"

"Is something the matter?" His whiskers bristled with suspicion.

"I've—*hic*—got the—*hic*—hiccups."

Mr. Ratnose surveyed the room. My classmates were watching.

"Well, why don't you go get a drink of water?" he said.

"O—*hic*—kay, teacher."

That was almost too easy.

Once outside, I made for Maureen DeBree's office. Ms. DeBree was Emerson Hicky's head custodian, a spic-and-span mongoose with a grudge against grime.

Ms. DeBree would have what I needed—not only the master key for all lockers, but a list of who had each one. I smiled. Bert Umber's locker would soon be an open book—er, locker.

Bap-bap-bap!

I rapped on her office door. It swung open.

"Well, if it ain't the private eyeball himself," she rasped. "Whassup?"

Her office reeked of ammonia and lemons. I gave it the once-over, noticing the framed Mr. Clean photo, the labeled keys hanging neatly in a row.

"I need some information."

"What, I look like a public library?"

"More like a bookmobile," I said. "Ms. DeBree, I'm after some stolen goods that might be stashed in a locker. Do you have a list of the locker assignments?"

Ms. DeBree eyed me. "Yeah."

I gave her my Jumbo Sincere-o smile. "Can I . . . take a peek at it?"

The mongoose swished her bushy tail and chewed on a Q-tip swab. "*Mmm,* I don't know . . . ," she said.

"Pleeeease." I gave her Bambi eyes, which usually works on my mom.

The head custodian cocked her head, considering. I sweetened the pot.

"I'll bring you some home-baked mealworm cookies."

"Hokey-dokey," she said.

Ms. DeBree pulled a file from her desk drawer. She paused.

"I dunno if this is a bona-fried, legal thing," she said, "so I'm gonna leave this file on my desk and go check for stray rubbish. If your eyeballs, *accidental-like,* read the file . . ."

"No one will know."

Maureen DeBree put a finger to her lips. "Strictly *shush-shush,*" she said, and strolled out the door.

I sprang to the desk and flipped open the folder. Running my finger along names, I muttered, "Let's see . . . Uvula . . . Urkle . . . Umber!"

Bingo: *Locker 337.* My eyes strayed to the rack. A shiny brass key hung under the label, MASTER KEY—LOCKERS.

Hmm. She'd probably say no if I asked to borrow it, but what if I just borrowed it *without* asking?

A footstep scuffed just outside the door.

Za-thwip!

Without thinking, I shot out my tongue and snagged the key—just in time.

"Funny t'ing," said Ms. DeBree, stepping into the office. "No trash in the hall."

I kept my mouth shut while she closed the folder and refiled it. The brass tasted bitter on my tongue.

The mongoose looked up. "You finished?" she asked.

"Mmm-hmm," I said, moving toward the door.

"Got whatcha needed?"

"Mmm-hmm."

She waved. "Laters."

"Mmm-kay." I zipped out the door and down the hall.

Ptah! Safely away, I spat the key into my palm. *Yuck.* What I really needed was a Sowbug Twinkie to chase away the aftertaste. . . .

But duty came first. I strolled past banks of lockers, looking for Bert's. Ah, good ol' number 337—right by the drinking fountain.

I glanced both ways. A dirt-brown prairie dog scurried around the corner, spotted me, then darted back into a classroom. The coast was clear.

One quick turn of the key, and the mysteries of Bert's locker lay revealed.

A chewed-up baseball sat atop a pile of random junk. I found old book reports, stinky sneakers, a

school photo of Lili Padd, more papers, and a half-eaten Lice Krispies bar.

Hmmm.

Munching on the candy, I sorted through the stack. Near the bottom was—well, well—an envelope covered with pink hearts. I wolfed down the rest of the treat and, holding the envelope by an edge, carefully opened it with a pencil.

When I turned it upside down, out fell . . . a valentine card. Its front featured a hairy creature with hearts all around it.

I peeked inside.

Friends like you are fur-ever! it read. *Be mine, valentine!* The card was signed, *Love, Sal.*

Eew. Mushy stuff.

Wait a minute. *Love, Sal?* I searched the locker again. No more valentines.

Piling everything back into place and closing the locker, I felt a funny pressure in my gullet.

"Hic!"

I went to the drinking fountain and slurped some water.

"Hic!"

I held my breath as long as I could and let it out.

"Hic!"

Great. Just great.

I gave up and headed back to class. Mr. Ratnose was going to just love this.

6

Freddie Nostrils

Ah, recess. Recess is the chocolate center of a Centipede Joy candy bar. Recess is school's way of letting kids blow off steam so they don't drive their teachers *loco*. (Too bad it never works.)

Afternoon recess found me huddling with Natalie over our next move. I told her what I'd found in Bert's locker.

Natalie groomed her feathers. "Shouldn't we check on his girlfriend Sally?" she said. "Maybe she swiped Lili's valentine."

"My money's still on Bert. But you're right; let's split up and track her down. First, get her full name."

Natalie saluted. "See ya later, investigator."

The clock was ticking. I hotfooted it for the upper-graders' playground.

Rounding a runculous tree, I jumped like a stuck frog when I found myself face-to-face with a dirt-brown prairie dog.

He bowed slightly. "Mr. Chet Gecko?"

"Yeah?"

"Allow me to introduce myself," he said. "I am Freddie Nostrils."

"Big whoop," I said. "Look, Slim, I'm in a hurry. No time for autographs."

I made to slip around him. Freddie blocked my path. I sized him up.

He would never make the Rodent Hall of Fame. Freddie's bulging eyes flanked a nose that looked like it'd blow off with a stiff sneeze. His overbite concealed a chin so weak, the nose could've beat it up.

Freddie's skinny body twitched like a silkworm in a light socket. He looked familiar, but if we'd met before, I'd thankfully forgotten.

"Make your pitch or make tracks," I said. "I'm a gecko with places to go."

Freddie Nostrils wrung his hands and offered up the most insincere smile I've seen outside of a parent-teacher conference.

"I would like to, er, talk to you about a matter of mutual interest," he said in a voice oilier than greaseball soup. "It concerns the Malted Falcon."

I snorted. "The moldy falcon? Who's that, some birdie's funky old grandma?"

The prairie dog sniffed. "Not moldy, *malted,*" he said. "You mean you don't know?"

I shook my head. "What's the Malted Falcon?"

"Er, think of the biggest dessert you can," said Freddie Nostrils.

"You don't know Chet Gecko," I said. "I can think of a pretty big dessert."

And I did. With pleasure.

Watching me, the prairie dog smirked. "Now triple it."

My eyes grew wide, picturing mountains of chunky weevil ice cream topped with snowcapped peaks of whipped cream. Candied grasshoppers did lazy backstrokes in lakes of fudge.

I think I started to drool.

"Er, Mr. Gecko?" he said. "Still with me?"

"Uh-huh."

"Excellent. Now, imagine having this dessert once a week . . . for a full year."

I blinked. "That's heaven."

Freddie leaned toward me. "No, it's not," he said. "That's the Malted Falcon."

"I don't understand."

The nervous rodent paced. "You know that candy shop at the mall . . ."

"Sweet Thang?"

I knew the joint. They'd tossed me out the

month before when I drank an entire Humungoloid Shake single-mouthed and danced the magic chicken mambo on the countertop.

Some shopkeepers don't appreciate the fine arts.

"Yes, er, Sweet Thang," said Freddie, derailing my train of thought. "They have been giving out tickets to win the Malted Falcon whenever you buy a dessert. A, er, friend of mine in Ms. Reckonwith's class got the winning ticket."

I swallowed my jealousy. "Lucky friend."

"Yes and no," he said.

"What do you mean?"

Freddie's buckteeth bared in a tight grin. "She, er, lost the ticket."

"Tough break," I said. "But what's all this got to do with me?"

The prairie dog fixed me with a bug-eyed stare. "I would like to hire you to find the missing ticket."

I was tempted, but . . . "Sorry, I've already got a case."

Freddie stepped closer. "I will double your fee," he said.

Double my already-doubled fee would buy me another Humungoloid Shake or two (if I could get back into Sweet Thang). *Mmm.*

"Freddie," I said, "I'm your gecko."

"Excellent!"

"When do I begin?"

The prairie dog reached into his book bag. His paw emerged holding a wicked-looking rubber-band gun. Loaded.

"How about right now?" said Freddie.

"What?"

He leveled the gun on me. "Hands up, please. We will start by searching *you* for the ticket."

7

It's All Geek to Me

The Detective Handbook says when a client pulls a rubber-band gun, you've got three choices: jump him, die of embarrassment, or go along with it. I went along with it. Freddie's twitchy trigger finger made me edgy.

Besides, I didn't *have* the winning ticket for the Malted Falcon. And I knew I'd pay Freddie back later, when he least expected it.

We finished our little charade. Freddie apologized, paid me a hefty retainer fee, and I beat feet for the upper-graders' playground. With a little luck, I could get a line on Bert's girlfriend Sal, before the—

Rrring!

Drat. My luck was in the repair shop, along with

my grade point average and my secret decoder ring. Recess ended. Detective work would have to wait.

Shuffling back to class, I considered my caseload. On the one hand: Find a missing valentine. On the other hand: Recover the ticket to the most awesome dessert ever.

Three guesses as to which case I liked best. (And the first two guesses don't count.)

Back in Mr. Ratnose's room, I endured our twice-weekly music lesson from Zoomin' Mayta, a hummingbird with a hyperactive sense of rhythm. If I had a musical bone in my body, Ms. Mayta hadn't found it yet.

When the last bell rang, I shot through the doorway like snot through a single-ply tissue. I caught Natalie at her classroom door. Amanda Reckonwith, her teacher, was chatting with a small pack of nerds inside while Natalie listened.

"What do you know?" I asked, pulling my partner's wing.

"An excellent joke," she said.

"Oh, joy."

Natalie's eyes glittered. "Two Eskimos were paddling their kayak when they got cold. One lit a fire in the canoe, and down it sank. Know what that proves?"

I braced myself. "What?"

"That you can't have your kayak and heat it, too!" she crowed.

I bit my lip. Natalie's puns can be deadlier than the aftereffects of bean-and-beetle burritos in a sleeping bag.

She stopped laughing long enough to fill me in on Sally. "Her last name's Monella," she said. "But I couldn't find her. We'll have to grill her tomorrow."

"Never mind that; we've got a second case."

"A *second* case?"

Natalie listened to the lowdown on Freddie Nostrils and the winning ticket for the Malted Falcon.

She cocked her head. "Let me get this straight," she said. "Freddie's friend had the winning ticket in class today."

"That's right."

"And somebody stole it."

"Yup."

She groomed a wing feather thoughtfully. "You know what I think?" asked Natalie.

"That the cafeteria should serve inchworm salad every day?"

"Besides that. The culprit's got to be someone in my class."

"Makes sense."

Natalie frowned. "Who was Freddie's friend, the one who lost the ticket?"

"He didn't say," I said. "But he sure wants it bad."

Just then, the doorway to Ms. Reckonwith's class filled with teacher's pets bound for home. Natalie looked at me.

"What are we waiting for?" she said.

I waved at the four geeks walking out. "Hey there, sports fans," I said. "Got a minute?"

A bespectacled pigeon blinked. "No, my good lizard, but I can spare exactly sixty thousand milliseconds."

I rolled my eyes at Natalie.

"Stop showing off, Henry," she said. "He's got a minute."

Hands on hips, I surveyed Natalie's classmates. Besides Henry the pigeon, we'd collared a roly-poly wombat and two sleek skinks.

"Any of you heard of the Malted Falcon?" I asked.

Four hands went up.

"One of your classmates got the winning ticket."

A chorus of *oohs* greeted that remark.

"Who won?" asked the wombat.

"We don't know," said Natalie. "But somebody else stole the ticket today."

"I suspect that Freddie character," said Henry, looking down his beak. "He's so deeply shifty."

Couldn't argue with him there. But Freddie was the client, not the thief.

"Did you notice anything odd in class today?" I asked.

The four kids exchanged glances. "Well," said the wombat, "Ms. Reckonwith wouldn't let me clap the erasers . . ."

"Um," said a skink. "I think Randy was cheating on the math quiz."

I tapped my foot. Witnesses like these wouldn't notice a brontosaurus in their cornflakes.

The other skink screwed up her face. "We, um, didn't get as much homework as I wanted."

Henry nodded. "Oh, yes, and Paige Turner went home in the middle of the day."

I sighed. "Was anyone snooping through someone else's things?"

All four shook their heads. I turned away.

"Okay," said Natalie. "You can go."

As they left, Henry the pigeon said, "I trust our recollections have been useful."

My smile was tighter than a rhino's bikini. "You'll never know how much, Henry boy."

I scoped out the school yard. Nearly everybody had gone, except for a couple of beefy muskrats hanging at the corner of the building. When they saw me looking, the pair began whistling and sauntered off.

Hmm. Sounded like someone else was flunking Zoomin' Mayta's music lessons.

Natalie and I peeked into her classroom. Nobody home but Amanda Reckonwith. I started through the door.

Natalie stopped me. "Never bother Ms. Reckonwith when she's grading papers," she said. "Trust me."

We made for the school gate. The campus had that peaceful feeling it gets when nobody's left but a few shell-shocked teachers and the kids in detention.

"So," I said, "no one to cross-examine."

"Nothing we can search," said Natalie.

I scratched my head. "What's left?"

Our eyes met. "Snack time at my house?" she asked.

"Partner," I said. "You're singing my song."

8

Surly in the Morning

Grade-school private eyes have it rough. For some reason, teachers won't give time off to fight crime, so you have to use your free time—at recess, lunch, and after school.

Sometimes you even have to snoop *before* school. *Yuck.*

The way I see it, mornings were meant for sleeping, not sleuthing. But with two cases on my plate, I set the clock for the crack of dawn.

The alarm blasted me out of a dream about the Malted Falcon. Good thing, too—I had eaten half of my pillow.

I staggered into school to find my early-bird partner waiting by the flagpole, whistling a tune. She looked as cheery as a snotbug in a booger factory.

"Good morning, sunshine," she trilled.

"Can the cheer," I grunted. "Let's snoop."

Natalie led the way to Bert Umber's classroom. If Lili's valentine wasn't in his locker, it might be in his desk.

As we walked, Natalie said, "You'll never guess what I saw on TV last night."

"Let's see . . . SpongeBird SquareBeak?"

"Nope, it has to do with one of our cases."

I shrugged.

"Give up?" she said. "The news report said that the winner of the Malted Falcon contest has to turn in the ticket by tonight."

"So if we don't find out who took it by then . . ."

"Bye-bye, big fat fees."

I shook my head. "Nothing like a deadline to focus the mind."

Up ahead, the windows of Bert's room were already lit. *Dang.* We'd have to use trickery to get past his teacher. I peeked through a windowpane.

Propped against a desk overflowing with papers sat Al LeGator, a portly crocodile with a pencil-thin mustache. (Don't ask me how a reptile could grow one; I don't want to know.) Scuttlebutt said he was an old softy, but Mr. LeGator was still a teacher and hard to fool.

"How do we get him out of there?" I whispered to Natalie.

She smirked. "Leave it to me."

In a voice like Principal Zero's she called out, "Mr. LeGator! I need to see you right away."

Man, those mockingbirds sure can mock.

"Eh?" The big crocodile lurched to his feet, peering about. "Mr. Zero? Where are you?"

I glared at Natalie. She had forgotten to imitate a loudspeaker first.

"Uh, I'm outside," she said. "No time to waste. Come to my office, now!"

Mr. LeGator waddled for the door—surprisingly fast for a bowlegged croc.

I glanced around. Too late to seek cover.

Fa-zip! I scuttled up the wall. In my line of work, it pays to be a lizard.

Natalie flapped frantically, just clearing the roof by the time Al LeGator's snout poked out the door. She threw her voice.

"Step smartly!" Principal Zero's words seemed to come from around the corner. "Haven't got all day."

Bert's teacher followed the voice, dragging his scaly tail behind him.

I slipped down the wall and through the door.

Mr. LeGator's classroom looked like a trash bomb had exploded. Junk overflowed the wastebaskets, old drawings were pinned three deep to the walls, and the stink of stale milk filled the air.

Using all my skills and the sweet science of

detection, I located Bert's desk. I flipped up the top and dug inside. It was worse than his locker.

Stacks of homework assignments that had never gone home. Toy soldiers, trading cards, and—one layer deeper—an emergency stash of barbecue-flavored grubworms.

Rats. Stale.

What a mess. Too bad I'd left my earthmover in my other jacket.

I searched quickly. Who knew how long Natalie could mislead Al LeGator?

Scuff, scuff, scuff.

Not long, apparently. Footsteps shuffled outside. I closed the desktop and leaped away from Bert's desk. Casually leaning against the wall, I smiled at . . .

Bert?

The marmot dragged into class. His face was puffier than a blowfish with the mumps. One eye was swollen almost shut. Fur was missing from his hide.

"Wow," I said. "What happened?"

He squinted at me. "Oh, I, uh . . . ran into a pole," he said.

"Looks like the pole won."

Bert mumbled something and limped toward his desk.

"Who did this to you?" I asked.

"Uh, nobotty. It vas . . . my fault."

Bert was a better basketball player than he was a liar. But I had no time to grill him further. A bulky figure filled the doorway.

"Well, hello," rumbled Al LeGator. "And what are you up to, pray tell?"

Bert hung his head. "I vas just—"

"Not you," said the potbellied crocodile, waddling into the room. "You." His heavy-lidded eyes fixed me with a friendly stare.

My tail curled.

"Me?" I edged around the desks. "I was, er, curious about fifth grade."

Mr. LeGator turned to watch me. "And?"

I flashed a quick grin. "Think I'll stay in fourth. We have a better dental plan, and the snacks are to die for."

"Hmm." The crocodile stroked his mustache.

At the door, I tipped my hat. "As the tree said to the bush, it's time for me to leaf." I made tracks.

Down the hall, Natalie was waiting.

"Sorry I couldn't keep him longer," she said. "Did you learn anything?"

"Yeah. Bert's hiding something, and it's not his charm and good taste."

"Why do they lie?" said Natalie. "We always find out."

"Beats me, birdie. Beats me."

9

Me and My Shadows

Math class is the zit on the nose of my school day. I've never liked it. Still, Mr. Ratnose's drone made for a pleasant background noise as I pondered my cases.

Who had beaten up Bert? Did it have to do with Lili's valentine? And how the heck were we going to interview all of Natalie's classmates and find the Malted Falcon ticket by tonight?

"Chet Gecko?" said Mr. Ratnose.

"Yes, teacher."

"The answer is . . . ?"

"Uh, can I get back to you?"

Mr. Ratnose pulled on his whiskers. "Honestly! Why do you always daydream during math class?"

"I wasn't daydreaming," I said. "I was having an out-of-body experience."

My teacher snorted and moved on to the next victim.

When recess rolled around, I trotted to Natalie's classroom. We'd planned to spend the time interviewing her classmates.

Luck was with me. As I slipped into the classroom, the snapping turtle, Ms. Reckonwith, was just closing her book.

"That's all for now," she said. "You may all go to recess—quietly."

Her students closed their books like good little boys and girls and got ready to go. They really toed the line in Reckonwith's class.

I strolled up to Natalie. "Let's get hopping."

"Like a pan full of popcorn," she said.

We asked several kids to wait a minute. For my first interview subject, I chose a sharp-faced dove in the back row.

"Hi, I'm Natalie's friend, Chet. We're working on a case."

"Oh, yeah?" she said.

"Yeah," I said. "And I was just wondering..."

My gaze wandered to Lili Padd, who was standing by the door. She shot me a big-eyed look. Of course, being a frog, most of her looks were big-eyed.

Lili mouthed, "Let's talk at lunch." I nodded.

"Wondering what?" said the dove.

"Hmm?" I asked.

She gathered up her books. "What were you wondering? Recess doesn't last forever."

"Uh, wondering if you saw anything suspicious..."

Someone bumped me—hard. I caught the dove's desk to keep from falling.

"Oops," said Little Gino, the oversized tuatara. "Did I hurt you, mate?"

It was déjà vu, all over again. "Not as much as that lobotomy must've hurt you," I said.

But before Little Gino and I could continue our tough-guy dance, Ms. Reckonwith called him to the front of the room.

"When?" asked the dove.

"What?" I said.

She sighed. "When did I see something suspicious?"

"You saw something suspicious?"

The dove shook her head. "You were asking me, remember?"

"Oh, right!" I leaned forward. "Yesterday, someone stole . . ."

Something tugged at my sleeve.

I turned, clenching a fist. "Would you just—"

Freddie Nostrils held up his paws. "No need for alarm, Mr. Gecko," he said. "I merely wanted to request a, er, lunch meeting to discuss my case."

"Oh." I blinked. "Okay."

Freddie joined the other kids trooping out the door.

"What?" It was the dove again.

"What *what*?"

"You haven't even asked me a question yet," she said. "What kind of detective are you?"

I scratched my head. "Sister, I've been wondering that myself."

Without further fuss, I interviewed the dove and a couple of other kids. By then, everyone else had hit the playground, except the teacher.

"Any luck?" I asked Natalie.

"Not yet," she said. "But we've got about six more kids to go."

"A-*hem*!" A sound like a buzz saw clearing its throat grabbed my attention.

Amanda Reckonwith sent a steely gaze through her spectacles. "Still here?" she said. "Isn't there somewhere else you have to be?"

"Um, yes, ma'am," said Natalie.

"Then *be there*!" Ms. Reckonwith snapped. Of course, you expect that from a snapping turtle.

We traipsed out the door to continue our interviews. As we headed for the playground, I scanned the halls for Natalie's classmates. No stragglers remained. Just a couple of big muskrats leaning on a wall, looking our way.

Big muskrats?

I muttered, "Don't look now, but we're being followed."

"Where?"

"Two hefty rodents, off the port bow."

She sneaked a quick glance. "Why are they after us?"

I picked up the pace. "Dunno. I spotted them yesterday after class, and now here they are again."

"Maybe it's your animal magnetism," she said.

"Very funny."

I began skipping. Natalie looked at me like I was cracked.

"Are they skipping?" I asked.

She checked. "Uh-huh. But they might have spring fever."

I started to trot. The shaggy duo trotted behind.

"Only one way left to be sure they're tailing us," I said.

"What's that?" Natalie flapped her wings to keep up.

"Run!"

So we ran, full tilt boogie. Behind us, footsteps echoed.

Natalie and I shot down the hall and around a corner. Before our pursuers appeared, I pointed up. Natalie flapped to the roof. I scrambled after her.

"What—" she started to say.

"Shh." I stopped her. Dropping to my belly, I peeked over the edge.

Two fuzzy heads met my gaze.

"Where'd they go?" said the frizzy-haired one.

"Search me," said the other, who had a head as round as a doughnut.

"Mr. Big ain't gonna like this," said Frizzy. "You blew our cover."

Doughnut Head whined. "Me? You're the one who kept staring at them like they was fresh cattail pie."

Still arguing, the pair stomped off down the hall.

I sat back on my heels. "You know what that means, don't you, when someone named Mr. Big is involved in a case?"

"Big trouble?" said Natalie.

"You can say that again."

"Big trouble?" she repeated.

I winced. "On second thought, once was enough."

10

Dustup with a Dunderhead

We had just enough time to grill someone before class. Natalie and I wandered the playground, checking for classmates we'd missed.

Then we hit the jackpot.

Little Gino leaned on a tetherball pole. He was uglier than a year without summer vacation.

"Hmm," I said. "He's big enough to be Big, and he could've stolen the ticket."

"Think you can make nice with him?" asked Natalie.

"No problem," I said. "I'm as mellow as Jell-O."

"Uh-huh. Jalapeño pepper Jell-O."

We stopped a few paces away from him.

Gino eyed us. "You lookin' for a knuckle sandwich?" he sneered.

I forced a smile. "No, thanks, not hungry. Look, maybe we got off on the wrong foot. Let's start again. I'm Chet Gecko; welcome to our school."

"Hah! I'm Little Gino; mind your own bizzo if you don't want a fat lip."

Natalie stepped in. "We just wanted to chat," she said. "That's all."

The tuatara rolled his shoulders. "Oh, yeah? What about?"

"Oh, things," she said.

"What things?"

"Things happening in your classroom," I said.

He frowned. "Keep your beak outta my room."

"Easy, big fella," said Natalie. "It's my room, too."

I watched a fly circle above the tuatara's head. "We just wondered if you saw anything odd yesterday, like someone where they shouldn't be?"

"Or something going missing?" Natalie added.

"What?" said Little Gino. "You calling me a thief?"

"Relax, Lumpy," I said. "No one's accused you of anything."

The tuatara noticed the fly. As he opened his mouth to slurp it up, I shot out my tongue and zapped it. That'd teach him to mess with Quick-Draw Gecko.

Little Gino snarled. "You think you're so hot."

"Only when it's sunny," I said.

His knobby spines seemed to rise. "Gecko, you've rubbed me the wrong way ever since I met you."

My eyes narrowed. "Believe me, there's no rub lost between us."

"That's it!" he snapped. "One more wisecrack, mate . . ."

Little Gino glared down at me. I glared back at him.

R-r-rring!

The bell kept him from having to finish his threat. (That, and a nearby teacher on yard duty.)

"Aw, get knotted, you Froot Loop!" he said. The tuatara stomped off.

Natalie raised her eyebrows. "Mellow as Jell-O, eh?"

"Hey, he's a touchy guy," I said.

We shuffled back to class. Sweaty kids tromped off the playground beside us. I paused at the corner of my building.

"Do me a favor, Natalie?"

"As long as it doesn't involve loaning you snack money."

I nodded at her classroom. "Keep an eye on Little Gino," I said. "He's up to something."

"Stealing the Malted Falcon ticket?"

"Dunno. But it's not running for Mr. Congeniality."

Natalie saluted me with a wing feather. "Righty-o, Gecki-o."

I nodded. "Pip-pip, No-Lips."

11

Out of the Frying Pan, into the Liar

I won't bother telling you about my classes before lunch (mostly because I can't remember them). Let's just say I came, I pretended to study, I left. And the whole time, I brooded on my cases.

Questions chased each other like pond skaters around the frozen swamp of my brain. Who stole the Malted Falcon ticket? Why was the mysterious Mr. Big interested in us? Who was he?

And, if aluminum foil is made of aluminum, what do they make foghorns out of?

Hungry for answers, I settled for lunch. Natalie and I polished off our creamed chipped beetles on toast and ambled over to the scrofulous tree to plan. Although both of our clients wanted a lunch meeting, neither one had said where.

As it happened, they came to us.

I'd just settled against the tree trunk when the bushes rustled. A lean prairie dog crawled out.

"Ah, Mr. Gecko and Ms. Attired," said Freddie Nostrils. "So good of you to meet me."

"What's on your mind, Freddie?" I asked.

He paced on the grass. "Er, the case," he said. "Have you made any progress in finding my, er, friend's ticket?"

"Not much," I said. We brought him up-to-date.

Freddie grimaced. "Can't you speed things up? My friend needs the, er, ticket by tonight."

"More information might help," I said. "For example, who is your friend?"

The prairie dog's eyes went wide. "Er, no. He wishes to stay anonymous."

"So he's a mouse?" asked Natalie.

"I didn't say that," Freddie said.

I stood up. "Wait, I thought your friend was a *she*."

"Did I say that?" Freddie looked past me and flashed a bucktoothed smile. "Hurry up and find the ticket," he said. "Time flies like an arrow."

"Yeah, and fruit flies like a banana," I said. "Why can't you—"

But before I could finish, Freddie Nostrils had popped out of sight.

Natalie looked where he'd gone. "As the mama

fish said when her husband was hooked, what's gotten into him?"

Just then, the bushes on the other side of the tree swayed. Lili Padd poked her froggy face around a clump of leaves.

"What is this," I said, "National Bush Creeping Day?"

"Have you found my valentine?" she asked hopefully.

"Not yet," said Natalie.

I scratched my chin. "Far as we know, Bert doesn't have it. We'll check on his girlfriend next."

Lili looked confused.

"His *other* girlfriend," said Natalie.

"Ah," said the frog.

Leaves crunched again, and we all turned to look. Freddie Nostrils was brushing twigs from his fur, saying, "What I *can* tell you is—"

He spotted Lili and stopped. Her mouth fell open.

"You!" they said together.

She hopped toward Freddie. He glanced at Natalie and me, then sidled up to the frog.

"My, my," he said. "It seems we are on the, er, same track."

"Could be," said Lili.

"Making any progress?" asked the prairie dog.

"Possibly," said Lili. She was cagier than the Three Blind Mice in a kitchen appliance store. But why?

"Does *he* know what you're doing?" asked Freddie.

"*He* who?" said Lili.

Natalie cocked her head and grinned. "He who lies down with dogs gets up with fleas!"

Both of our clients just stared at her. Sometimes, I don't get mockingbird humor, either.

"You know who," said Freddie. "Mr. Big."

Lili glared at the prairie dog. "Not in front of my detective," she hissed.

"He's *my* detective," said Freddie. "I hired him first."

"Nuh-uh, I did."

Strange—I was suddenly Mr. Popularity. If only my teachers felt this way.

I stepped forward. "Wait a minute," I said. "Who is Mr. Big? And why would he care about you getting your valentine back?"

Freddie stared at Lili. *"Valentine?"* he said. "Then you have not told th—"

"That's enough!" said the frog. She shoved Freddie with both webbed feet.

Whomp! He staggered back into the tree.

I grabbed Lili's arm. "Told us what?" I asked.

"Nothing!" she said.

Freddie grinned a crooked grin. "She is after the same thing I am: the Malted Falcon ticket."

His words sank in. I released Lili.

Natalie gaped. "You—you lied to us *again*!?"

Lili shrugged. "I'm not proud of it."

"Enough!" I said. "I don't have to take this kind of abuse from a client; that's why I've got a little sister."

I nodded to Freddie. "From now on, we've only got *one* client. Come on, Natalie."

We started to go.

"But—" said the frog.

"No froggy buts," I said.

Freddie smoothed his fur. "Perhaps we should discuss joining forces?"

Lili's wide mouth began to tremble, and her huge eyes glistened. She caught my sleeve.

"Please, Chet. Just a word before you go?"

A tear quivered on her lower eyelid.

"All right," I said. "What harm could one word do?"

12

Skip to My Loser

Five minutes later, we'd made a deal. Natalie and I promised to give Lili one more chance, and she promised to work with Freddie. Lili paid us a bonus. And she gave us a tip—the Malted Falcon ticket was inside a valentine.

But neither she nor Freddie would say anything more about Mr. Big.

I didn't worry; I had my own ideas about reaching him.

Natalie and I left our clients and hustled off to find Bert's girlfriend Sally Monella. If she didn't have the envelope, we faced a lot more legwork.

We hadn't gone far when I got a tingly feeling. (No, not gas.) A casual look around revealed the two muskrats who had shadowed us earlier.

Natalie had spotted them, too. "We've got company," she said.

"Darn, and I forgot to wash the good china."

"Shall we lose 'em?"

"No," I said. "I've got a better idea."

I whispered it, then quickened my step. The muskrats stuck close behind.

"This way!" I said.

Natalie and I ducked behind a portable building. We turned a corner. But rather than trying to lose them, we doubled straight back—into our pursuers.

The look on their faces was priceless.

"Oh! Uh," said Doughnut Head, "nice day for a stroll, huh?"

"Yeah," Frizzy seconded. "Fancy meeting you guys here."

I planted my hands on my hips. "Cut the comedy," I said. "We know why you fuzzballs are following us."

Frizzy looked like he'd been caught with a fist in the fudge tray. His brows furrowed. "Umm . . ."

"Try 'I don't know what you're talking about,'" Natalie prompted.

"Thanks," he said. "I don't know what you're talking about."

Doughnut Head punched his buddy's arm. "Come on, man. They *know.*"

"That's right," I said. "And we want to meet Mr. Big."

The muskrats looked blankly at each other. Obviously, their henchman training hadn't included independent thinking.

"I dunno," said Doughnut Head.

"Don't you think Big will want to meet someone who's got what he wants?"

"Yeah, but—" said Frizzy.

"Then tell him: four o'clock sharp, behind the library."

Natalie and I left the muskrats behind, scratching their heads.

"Do we really have what he's looking for?" she asked.

"What do you think?"

"I think you like living dangerously," said Natalie.

"Danger is my middle name," I said.

Natalie smirked. "I thought it was Humperdink."

"Shh."

During my brief stint on the football team (don't ask), I got to know the cheerleaders better than any gecko should. Sal Monella, the kangaroo rat, was a cheerleader's cheerleader. Odds were, she'd be at the gym with the rest of them.

I never get tired of being right.

In the shadow of the gymnasium, two cheerleaders swung a pair of jump ropes. Two others skipped in and out and over in a pattern as complicated as a butterfly's bloomers. One of them was Sally.

They were singing as we approached.

> *"Hip, hop, skiddley widdley wop*
> *Girls are genius, come from Venus*
> *Boys are stupider, come from Jupiter"*

The scene was as full of cooties as a truant is full of lies. I would have to tread very, very carefully.

"You go first," I muttered.

"Bawk, bawk," said Natalie, in a pretty fair imitation of a chicken. She strolled up to the girls while I hung back.

"Hiya, ladies," she said.

They greeted Natalie with friendly twitters.

"Wanna jump?" asked Sal, her powerful hind legs pistoning.

"No, thanks," said Natalie. "Just wanted to ask a few questions."

Hopping lightly over the spinning ropes, the kangaroo rat flicked her eyes at my partner. "Okay. You want answers, you skip."

Her fellow jumper headed for the sidelines.

Natalie shrugged, then started skipping. "How well do you know Bert Umber?"

The rat tittered. "Oh, pretty well," she said. "Hello? He's my boyfriend."

Her pals giggled.

"We're trying to find something that he, um, borrowed from our client."

"Borrowed?" said Sal.

I stuck my two cents in. "Yeah," I said, "as in *stole.*"

"Who's your friend?" Sal asked my partner. "He looks familiar."

"Chet Gecko," said Natalie.

"Reeeally?" The rat tossed me a flirty look while her mighty hind legs kept jumping. She called out, "Well, Chet Gecko. If you wanna ask a question, you hafta skip, too."

"What?" I said.

"Ah-ah-ah," said Sal. "Skip first."

Yuck. I hoped my cootie shields would hold.

Skipping didn't look too hard. I stagger-stepped, then joined them.

"Okay, Sal, we're—*oop*—after something Bert had in a valentine envelope. Seen anything—*yike*—like that?" I asked, narrowly avoiding the ropes.

The kangaroo rat took her tail in one hand and swung it in a counter rhythm to the jump ropes. Show-off.

"I might have," she said coolly.

"Well, did you or didn't you?" said Natalie. "We—watch it, Chet!"

I twitched my tail out of Natalie's face. My feet barely cleared the rope. My breath was coming hard.

"The valentine came from his *other* girlfriend," I said.

Bad move.

Sal's eyes flashed red. "Double-time!" she snarled at the rope twirlers.

Skip-skip.

Skip-skip.

"You heard wrong!" she snapped, her feet a blur. "He doesn't have another girlfriend. Hello? Bert's nuts about me."

I was beginning to wonder exactly who was nuts. The cheerleaders spun the rope like a runaway top, faster and faster.

Skip-skip skip-skip.

Skip-skip skip-skip.

I was *boing*ing like a pogo stick to keep up while Natalie flapped her wings, hovering in the air. "Cheater!" I hissed.

She stuck out her tongue. "Come on, Sal," said Natalie, "did you see the envelope or not?"

"I did." She pouted. "And later, I talked to Bert about being a one-gal guy."

I remembered Bert's black eye and puffy face. Sal was one persuasive talker.

"Did you open the envelope?" I asked.

Skip-skip skip-skip.

Skip-skip skip-skip.

"Yeah," said Sal. "I wanted to see what *she* had to say to my Bert."

"Where's the envelope now?"

Sal turned up her nose. "The valentine was blank. I tore it up and threw it away."

I started to say, "And what else was—"

Skip-skip.

Skip-WHAP!

The rope caught on my tail. *"Whoa!"*

It neatly swung me in a loop, tootsies over hat. I admired the world from upside down, then—*whump!*—landed hard on a pile of rope skippers, bird, and rat.

The world hit the PAUSE button.

Someone stirred beneath me. With a groan, I rolled onto my side. I opened my eyes to find Sal Monella's smoochy lips just inches from my own.

Yikes! Cootie alert!

My reflexes took over. I jumped up. "Uh, it's been . . . something," I said. "See ya later."

"But . . . ," said Natalie.

"But . . . ," said Sal.

"But nothing," I said. "And if you'll excuse the crack, I'm butting out."

13

Never Been Tryst

When I returned to my trusty desk after lunch, something was different. A sixth sense told me someone had been snooping. Maybe it was the chocolate paw prints smeared on the desktop that tipped me off, or the fact that all my papers were scrambled.

Or maybe it was the small paper tag that read: THIS DESK INSPECTED BY NO. 563.

At least they take pride in their work, I thought.

I scoped out my classroom, but nobody slunk away guiltily or shouted out, *I confess!*

Sometimes detecting can be a challenge.

Rooting through my mess, I discovered nothing had been taken. . . . But wait!

Something lay inside the desk that hadn't been

there before: a frilly pink envelope with my name on it.

I bent close, sniffing carefully. It smelled faintly of strawberry perfume and dirt. Alert for a booby trap, I slit the envelope.

Be mine, Valentine? read the card inside.

After all that, a stinking mash note?!

My instincts said, trash the thing. I should've listened to my instincts.

Instead, I opened the card. In a round, girlish hand, the message read:

Dear Chet—

Roses are red
Garlic is stinkin'
Someone stoled the ticket,
But it ain't who you're thinkin'.

—Muchas smoochas,
a friend

P.S.: Meet me in the auditoryum <u>*alone*</u> *at three o'clock. I'll tell you the rest.*

It sure was nice to have a friend—especially one with clues. But what did he or she mean? Who was I thinkin' stole the ticket? Bert? Sally? Little Gino?

And was this note legit? Or was it just some

Valentine's Day ruse to get me alone and douse me with cooties? I eyeballed Shirley Chameleon, but she turned up her nose at me. Wasn't her.

Hmm. This was some mystery.

"Class, open your science books to page seventy-five," said Mr. Ratnose. "Let's discuss tectonic plates."

Almost as much of a mystery as how I'd get through an hour of science without having a nap attack.

Somehow, I managed to do my schoolwork. By the time the recess bell finished chiming, I was as long gone as Dad's tie-dyed bell-bottoms.

I dropped by Maureen DeBree's office to give her the cookies I'd promised. (And while she was busy with them, I returned the borrowed locker key.)

From there, this gecko hightailed it to Al LeGator's classroom. If Sal had tossed the valentine envelope, she might have tossed it in Mr. LeGator's wastebasket. After all, he was her teacher.

Natalie was waiting by the fifth graders' building.

"Why is it," she said, "that we always end up Dumpster diving for clues?"

"It's a glamorous life," I said.

Sometimes, detective work is harder than a sow-bug gingersnap straight from the freezer. And sometimes, Dame Fortune smiles on you like a parent at a straight-A report card. (Like I knew anything about *that*.)

We were lucky. Not only was Mr. LeGator tied up with yard duty, but also his classroom was dark and empty. Perfect for snooping.

"Keep a lookout," I told Natalie.

She watched for sneaky muskrats while I tried the doorknob. Locked. I guess Dame Fortune was only smirking.

Still, locked doors pose no problem for a detective with flexible morals. And it just so happens, I am that detective.

I poked the tip of my tail into the keyhole and wiggled it. After a few seconds, something gave.

Turning the knob, I felt the satisfaction of a successful lock picker . . . and—*ow!*—the pain of a pinched tail.

The door eased open, and we slipped into the room. The stale-milk smell had ripened. It was now strong enough to hold up the roof.

I cased the joint, searching for a wastebasket.

"Oh, look!" said Natalie, pointing to a corner.

"What? A clue?"

She smiled. "Nope, they're celebrating Bird History Month. Check out these cool dioramas." Natalie admired the students' handiwork.

I glanced at the row of boxes containing cardboard figures of famous birds.

"That's just peachy. Now, can you tear your eyes off Leonardo da Finchy long enough to help me?"

"Please, that's Mahawkma Gandhi," said Natalie.

I squinted at the box. It held a cutout of some serious-looking bird in a shawl—Mahawkma Gandhi, I guess. Big whoop.

"Okay, swami," I said. "Can we snoop now?"

We found the wastebasket under a rubbish landslide, sat down, and started digging. Several minutes later, we had unearthed brown apple cores, soggy tissues, scads of candy wrappers, bad poetry, worse English papers, and enough valentine envelopes to wallpaper Mount Rushmore and the girls' bathroom.

Clump-clompeda-clump!

At the sudden noise, we startled. What sounded like a herd of wildebeests tromped down the hall. But none of them came inside. We resumed working.

Natalie and I rummaged through valentine envelopes—some reeking with vile perfume, some smeared with cheap lipstick. It was enough to make your hair stand on end (if you had hair, which I don't).

But we didn't see any envelopes with Bert's name on them.

I was almost ready to throw in the towel when Natalie said, *"Hmm."*

"*Hmm* what?" I asked.

"Just *hmm.*"

She uncrumpled a pink envelope. Clumsy block letters spelled out *Bert + Lili.*

"Ah-ha!" I said.

"Nuh-uh," she answered. "Does that look like Lili's writing?"

I leaned closer. "Nope, it doesn't. And she told us it'd say *Lili + Bert.*"

Natalie opened the envelope and showed me what was inside. Nothing.

Rats. No Malted Falcon ticket. Visions of that stupendous dessert danced in my frustrated head.

"Hmm," I said.

"*Hmm,* indeed," said Natalie.

I tucked the envelope into my coat. We searched the area, but no tickets waved their little hands and sang out, *Here I am.*

"Maybe someone pocketed it." I scratched my chin. "Natalie, why don't we just—"

Rrring! went the bell.

"Scram?" she asked. "Good idea."

When the bird's right, she's right. We scrammed.

14

Ticket or Leave It

After the school day limped to a close, I hotfooted it over to Natalie's classroom. We were running as short on ideas as a ten-year-old TV sitcom. When we interviewed the last of her classmates, I'd be fresh out of leads.

And that's a bad place to be, when you're facing Mr. Big in just a couple of hours. Me and my big mouth.

Working quickly, we chatted up an opossum and a couple of crows. No luck. They had about as much useful information as a Pig Latin–Chinese dictionary.

The last stragglers tidied up their desks as Natalie and I compared notes.

"Who's left?" I asked.

"Paige Turner, the titmouse . . ."

"Why is she called a tit*mouse* when she's a bird?"

"It's a mystery," said Natalie. "And there's Bona Petite, that little French chick."

I gaped. "Natalie! Even *I* know you're not supposed to call girls *chicks*."

"Why not?" she said. "She's a chickadee."

I rolled my eyes. "Whatever. Let's get 'em."

Paige Turner was just heading out the door, a gloomy gray bird in a pink cashmere sweater.

I caught her wing. "Can I have a word?"

"Sure," she said, "if it's *sayonara*."

"Look, sister," I said. "My temper's shorter than a flea's jump rope, my patience is thinner than a first grader's lie, and I'm plumb out of time. Just answer my questions."

Her beak fell open. "Okay."

"Did anything unusual happen here yesterday?"

"Well, yes," she said.

"What?"

Paige's chin quivered. "M-my Malted Falcon ticket disappeared, and I c-can't find it anywhere."

The caboose of my brain collided with the engine of my theories in a major train wreck. Confusion spattered everywhere. It wasn't pretty.

I choked out, "Huh?"

"And if I d-don't find it by tonight, I'll miss out on a year's worth of dessert."

Paige looked bluer than a bandicoot on an ice-berg. She sniffed.

My brain struggled to get back on track. I shook my head.

"Hang on," I said. "*Your* Malted Falcon ticket?"

The titmouse pouted. "I got it two nights ago," she said. "But I brought it in for show-and-tell yesterday, and it disappeared."

"O-okay then, what's it look like?" I asked.

"A brown cardboard ticket shaped like a falcon, about so long." Paige indicated a wing feather. "I wrote my name on the back."

By then, Natalie had finished chatting with the chickadee and joined us.

I pointed at Paige. "*Her* Malted Falcon ticket."

Natalie stared at the titmouse, who nodded. My partner ruffled her feathers. "That Lili!" said Natalie. "When I get through with her . . ."

"But wait," I said. "How do we know Paige is on the up-and-up?"

"*Paige?!* What about *Lili*? She hasn't played straight since the beginning."

I held up my hands. "All right. No need to get feisty."

Paige coughed delicately. "Excuse me?" she said. "What are you talking about?"

We filled her in on the whole caper—how two

of her classmates had hired us to find the missing ticket. When we finished, she was bug-eyed.

"Well," said Paige, "I can't afford to bid for your loyalty. But I hope if you find it, you'll do the right thing."

"Absolutely!" said Natalie. "We—*mmf*—"

I clapped a hand around her beak. "We'll think about it," I said. "Come along, Natalie."

Just down the hall, we stopped.

"'We'll think about it'?" said my partner. "Come on, Chet. It's her ticket."

"Finders keepers. Besides, I don't think it's ethical to sell out our clients."

"Yeah, but it's *right*!" Natalie frowned. "And you know it."

I paced. "I don't know much. But I do know this: If we can't figure out where the ticket is before meeting Mr. Big, it doesn't matter who gets it."

"Why?"

"'Cause *we're* gonna get it."

15

Tea for Tuatara

My mind was racing like a cheetah on espresso. Which one of Natalie's classmates was telling the truth? Where was that ticket? Had we already interviewed the one who swiped it? My money was on Little Gino.

Speak of the devil.

As Paige walked past us, I saw beyond her a familiar lumpy reptile. The sweet-tempered tuatara himself, Little Gino.

"Come on, Natalie," I said. "We'll get a straight answer out of this crooked character, or my name's not Chet Gecko."

She followed. "I don't think he cares what your name is."

Arms crossed, the tuatara leaned against a wall. His sneer was so bad it had a sneer of its own.

"Let's talk turkey, turkey," I said.

"Gobble, gobble," said Little Gino.

"How come you're always lurking around?"

He looked me up and down. "How come *you* are, *mate*? This is my building."

Natalie cocked her head. "We're working on a case."

"Yeah?" said the tuatara. "Looked like he was workin' on suckin' up to that titmouse." He pushed off the wall and gave me the hairy eyeball.

"What?" I asked.

"Stay away from her, you drongo."

Suddenly, Natalie laughed. "I get it," she said. "He's sweet on Paige."

"Am not," Little Gino growled. His face turned three shades of red—not bad for a non-chameleon.

"*Aww.* Widdow Gino's got a widdow cwush on someone," I said.

Fooshhh! His punch passed harmlessly above me as I ducked.

I sprinted down the hall. "Thanks, Lumpy!" I shouted. "You just saved us a lot of investigative work."

The tuatara chased us awhile, but his heart wasn't in it. When we reached the library steps, Natalie and I slowed.

"What time is it?" I asked.

She glanced through the doors. "Almost three o'clock," said Natalie. "Why?"

"I've got a lead to follow."

She perked up. "I'll help."

"Naw, it's not that kind of lead." I didn't know why, but I felt too embarrassed to tell her about my valentine rendezvous. "Try to figure out where the ticket is and who has it. Meet you here just before four o'clock?"

"Okeydokey, artichokey," she said with a doubtful look.

I hustled down empty halls toward the auditorium. By now, the cafeteria ladies would've left. I half expected to find the building locked and deserted.

Who was I kidding? I *hoped* it'd be deserted. This whole "muchas smoochas" thing had my palms sweating like a penguin in a sauna. I reached for the door.

Click-eeeeeak.

It swung open.

"Hello?" I called into the dimness. "Um, friend?"

A faint aroma of floor wax and burnt grasshoppers hung in the air like the threat of rain. I stepped inside.

"Anybody home?" I said, tiptoeing between rows

of Formica-topped benches. When no reply came, I sighed. *Just a wild goose chase,* I thought.

"Over he-ere!" A girl's voice called from the front of the room.

My eyes strained, but I couldn't see anyone. I walked forward, row by row. Now I was just steps away from the stage and its moth-nibbled curtains.

"Where?" I asked. "I can't see you."

"Back he-ere." Closer now, the muffled voice came from behind the curtains.

I hopped onto the stage and fumbled with yards of heavy velvet. Why didn't they just paint a big arrow and an OPEN HERE sign on these suckers?

At last, I parted the curtains. "Okay," I said, sticking my head through the opening. "What've you got for me, valentine?"

A figure moved in the darkness. "This!" it said.

A rough sack slipped over my head. It stank of putrid potato bugs, skunk armpits, and something sickly sweet. Strawberries?

I reached for the sack, but four strong hands pinned my arms. The girl's voice said, "Sorry!" And—*whonk!*—something harder than a ten-page history test smacked me over the head.

Not as sorry as I am, I thought.

And the lights went out.

16

Big Business

Time flies when you're knocked out cold. Trust me. I know.

When the lights came on again, they were shining right in my face. *Too bright.*

I blinked. My head throbbed. Some heavy-handed hippo had been playing bongos with my skull. And while he was at it, he'd dipped my eyes in molasses.

I squinted into the glare of two sun-bright lamps. Shadowy figures drifted behind them. I found myself trussed to a chair, neat as you please.

"Welcome back, Sleeping Beauty," a deep voice rumbled.

I tried to turn my head. Two webbed paws grabbed it and kept me facing front. It seemed like I was in some kind of classroom, but where?

A ripe smell slapped my nose around, but I couldn't place it (the smell, not my nose).

"If you cooperate, this will all go much more smoothly," said Deep Voice. "You know why you're here, of course?"

"Uh, let me guess." My throat was as dry as a camel's crackers. "I made the semifinals of the detective roping contest?"

A chuckle came from behind the brightness. "Wonderful," said Deep Voice. "Ever the jokester. No, this is about the Malted Falcon ticket."

"Gee," I said. "Doesn't ring a bell."

"Do you remember calling this meeting in the first place?"

I shook my head to clear it. "Mr. Big?"

"Correct. Tell me what I need to know, and you can go back to your little gecko games."

The more he talked, the more familiar that voice became. I knew I'd heard it before. Looking down, I glimpsed candy wrappers and piles of papers.

"And what do you need to know?" I asked. "The phone number of a good interior decorator?"

Mr. Big paced slowly, accompanied by a dragging sound. That also seemed familiar. *Hmm.*

"The ticket, Gecko. Where is it?"

"Ah, that." I shifted against my ropes. "When I said I had it, I actually meant I knew where I could lay my hands on it."

Mr. Big stopped. "And where is that?"

My mind raced. How could I stall this big palooka?

"Uh, I'd have to lay hands on my partner first. She has that information."

Mr. Big let out a snort like a water buffalo inhaling a golf ball. "He's bluffing. Hit him with the board again."

"Please, not again," said a girl's voice behind me. Wait, I knew that voice.

"Lili?" I said.

She sighed. "Yes. But I'm not proud of it."

"And you'll recognize another of your 'clients,' too," said Mr. Big.

"Good afternoon, Mr., er, Gecko," came a voice behind the lights.

"Freddie Nostrils?"

"One and the same," said Freddie.

Mr. Big chuckled again. Quite the jolly villain. "You see, they're both in my employ. The irony is delicious."

Wait a minute—*both* my clients were working for the bad guy? I hoped this didn't get out. What would the other detectives say?

"Well?" said Mr. Big. "Time is running short, Gecko."

And finally, I placed his voice. "I never would have guessed a teacher was behind this," I said. "You can drop the act now, Mr. LeGator."

"Ah, well, I suppose you were bound to guess it sooner or later. All right, boys. Hit him."

Footsteps scuffed behind me.

"Wait!" I said. "You win."

Freddie Nostrils giggled. "I told you it, er, wouldn't take long."

I slumped. "Just untie me, and I'll show you where I have the ticket."

Mr. LeGator stepped forward and thrust his snout into my face. His breath enveloped me like a peppermint cloud.

"What kind of chump do you take me for?" he asked.

I had to bite my tongue to keep from jumping on that straight line.

"No kind of chump," I said. "I know when I'm licked. You got me surrounded; what am I gonna do? Make a break for it?"

Al LeGator looked me straight in the eye for a long moment. Then he chortled. Freddie and the unseen mugs behind me joined in.

"He's right," said the big crocodile. "What could he possibly do?"

At a sign from the boss, two pairs of hands untied my bonds. Twisting, I saw the two muskrats who'd been shadowing us. The ropes dropped away.

I stood and smiled. *Suckers.*

Hooking my tail around the chair leg, I gave a quick tug.

Kla-gonk!

The chair fell into one muskrat's knees, knocking him into the crocodile.

"Hey!" shouted Mr. LeGator.

Ba-whomp!

They went down like a duck after the last slice of pond-scum pie.

I bent under the other muskrat's grab and spun away from the lights. These crooks hadn't counted on my quick gecko reflexes.

Bwank! I barked my shin on a desk in the dark.

Stifling a scream, I limped down the aisle, making for the door.

"Stop him!" yelled Mr. LeGator.

The windows were shrouded with heavy blackout curtains, so I could barely make out the classroom. I skidded into a corner, where the door was supposed to be.

Whumf! I put my foot through a cardboard box. Stupid dioramas!

Wearing one like a shoe, I spun, dashed for the other corner—and pulled up short. Freddie Nostrils was waiting with arms wide. His buckteeth gleamed in the dimness.

I turned again.

Doughnut Head the muskrat was closing in on me.

I was trapped.

Like any self-respecting gecko, I jumped for the wall. I tried to scuttle up it, but the box on my foot made me slip. The burly muskrat reached for me, grinning.

"Hold it right there!" bellowed a voice. Principal Zero?

Conditioned by years of habit, the kids below me froze. I gently shook the box off my foot. Never had I been so glad to hear my principal's voice.

But where was he?

My captors were starting to wonder the same thing.

"If you're Principal Zero," said Mr. LeGator, "show yourself."

"Nuh-uh. You first," said the principal's voice. "March outside right now!"

"Nothing doing," said the crocodile.

I crawled along the wall toward the door. Just a few feet more . . .

When the principal didn't open it, Mr. LeGator said, "Pay no attention. Someone is imitating Zero—it happened to me earlier."

Freddie Nostrils jerked open the door, flooding the room with light. And there in the doorway stood my partner, Natalie Attired.

The lean prairie dog grabbed her wing, slung her inside, and slammed the door again. Great. Now we were both trapped.

"No more monkey business," said Mr. LeGator. "Are you going to give me that ticket, or shall I skin you both alive? Or do you want to get into some *real* trouble?"

And this, I knew, was one multiple-choice quiz I couldn't afford to flunk.

17

Bird to the Wise

When you're cornered by a criminal mastermind and the situation looks bleak, just remember: Things are darkest just before . . . they go completely black.

Or something like that.

True, Natalie and I were outnumbered, trapped inside a classroom with Mr. LeGator and his bigger, stronger crew. But on our side, we had . . . um . . . our wits.

Not fair.

Still, we couldn't surrender. Natalie paced warily between the muskrats and Freddie Nostrils, our fair-weather client. Lili and Al LeGator watched from between the rows of desks.

I crawled along the wall. Spotting a misshapen clay pot atop a cabinet, I dropped it on Freddie's noggin. *Take* that, *you dirty dog.*

"Ow!" The prairie dog staggered under the impact. He straightened and glared up at me.

Okay, maybe I couldn't get past Freddie's guard, but I could shed some light on the situation. I reached down with my tail and flicked on the light switch.

"Hey!" said Frizzy the muskrat, squinting. "That smarts."

Everyone blinked at the sudden light. Everyone except Natalie. She used the confusion to flap herself airborne and sail over the desks.

Mr. LeGator grabbed at her. "You'll never escape," he said. "Give up."

"Mrs. Gecko didn't raise no quitters," I said.

He winced. "Apparently, she didn't teach you proper grammar, either."

Natalie landed on Mr. LeGator's desk. While the crocodile focused on me, she pointed a wing feather at the telephone and made a face.

I saw her plan at once. "What say we call out for pizza?" I said.

Natalie rolled her eyes.

"I prefer sweets," said Mr. LeGator.

Behind him, Natalie had slipped the phone off the hook and was dialing, unnoticed.

"I'll just bet you do," I said. "Is that why you hatched this plan?"

Mr. LeGator smiled, a true crocodile smile. "I suppose I can tell you, since it'll be your word against ours. But after my story's done, you give me the ticket."

"No funny business," I promised.

Lili slumped into a chair. Freddie armed himself with a long pointer, and the muskrats lurked below me, guarding the door.

Al LeGator stroked his mustache. "Like you, Chet Gecko, I have my appetites." He patted his swollen belly. "But unlike you, I'm willing to do whatever it takes to satisfy them."

"Like stealing?" asked Natalie.

"Let's call it creative acquisition," said the crocodile. "I bought up all the desserts I could at Sweet Thang. And just in case, I created a network of informers to let me know if someone else won the Malted Falcon ticket."

I crawled along the wall toward Natalie. Freddie and Doughnut Head followed below. Mr. LeGator's long snout tracked me.

"So somebody squealed on Paige?" I asked.

"Her own best friend, in fact," he said. "But before I could take steps to acquire the ticket . . ."

"Steal it, you mean," I said.

He waved a thick, clawed hand. "If you wish. Lili

decided she wanted the ticket for herself. So she had Bert steal it before we could."

Lili hung her head. "Sorry," she mumbled.

"Not as sorry as you'll be if you get me for fifth grade," said Mr. LeGator.

I glanced at Natalie. The phone was still off the hook. Somebody was getting an earful.

"But Bert didn't give you the ticket, did he?" I asked Lili.

Her wide mouth turned down. "I thought he double-crossed me," she said. "That's when I hired you to find it."

Al LeGator cleared his throat. "And now I must ask you to hand it over."

I crawled down the wall. My brain was as empty of plans as a nerd's date book. Pretending to fumble in my coat for the ticket, I stalled once more.

"But why?" I asked.

Mr. LeGator's eyes took on a dreamy cast. "Since the discovery of sugar, we have quested for the perfect dessert. From the cookie to the cake, from the Popsicle to the sundae, we have searched. And now at last, it's here."

He thrust out a clawed hand. "And it's all mine. Give it!"

The jig was up. I reached into my pocket and pulled out . . . Lili's envelope?

Mr. LeGator snatched it. "At last!" he cried. The crocodile fumbled open the envelope. "Empty?"

"Hold it right there!" bellowed a voice that sounded a lot like Principal Zero's.

Mr. LeGator sneered and turned to Natalie. "Oh, please," he said. "I didn't fall for that last time. Why would I this time?"

Fa-tchoom!

The door burst open, revealing the real Principal Zero. "Because you, mister, are in deep, deep doo-doo."

"Wha-at?" Mr. LeGator turned an unnatural shade of white.

At a sign from the principal, Maureen DeBree and Vice Principal Shrewer strode into the room and rounded up the conspirators. The kids went quietly.

"You've got nothing on me," said the crocodile.

"On the contrary," said Mr. Zero. His claws unsheathed themselves. "I've had my eye on you. Ever since you came to this school, my office stash of Creamy Cockroach bars has been mysteriously disappearing."

The former Mr. Big forced a chuckle. "Nonsense," he said. "It could just as easily have been young Gecko over there."

"I thought so, too, at first," said the principal.

"But fourth-grader geckos don't leave size twelve footprints."

"Even if I did take your candy, that's not against the law."

"True enough," said Principal Zero. His tail twitched. "But I think the teacher's union would be very interested in your corrupting students and conspiring to steal. You, sir, are a very bad role model."

Mr. LeGator thrust his chest out. "Where's your proof?" he asked.

The principal pointed at the phone. "I heard every word. And I'm sure somebody here would testify to get out of lifelong detention."

Lili and Freddie wilted under his stare.

Beaten, Mr. LeGator and his gang slouched outside. Principal Zero nodded to us. "Much appreciated," he said, and followed them.

Natalie joined me at the back of the room. She surveyed the crushed dioramas, broken pottery, and scattered papers, and she shook her head. "What a mess."

"Worse than my bedroom," I said.

"But not by much."

We started pushing the rubbish into piles and setting the toppled chairs upright. It seemed like the least we could do.

"Well, that's that," said Natalie.

"Yup," I agreed. "Quick thinking, partner. But how did you find me?"

Natalie raised an eyebrow. "Good thing I got restless," she said. "I was walking the halls and thinking, when I saw our muskrat friends and Lili carrying something in a sack—something with a long green tail. I followed."

"I'm glad you did. You deserve a spot in the birdie hall of fame."

I picked up the Bird History diorama I'd stomped on earlier. It was the one with Mahawkma Gandhi. Carefully, I tried to straighten the box.

Natalie cocked her head. "But there's one thing I don't get."

"Hmm?"

"Where is that winning ticket?"

I couldn't answer. My attention had been captured by the diorama, by the brown birdie figure of Gandhi with its shawl askew. Something about it . . .

"Oh, Chet?" said Natalie.

I rotated the box in my hands. Natalie leaned closer and read its label, *"The Life of Mahawkma Gandhi, by Sally Monella."*

"What did Paige say that ticket looked like?" I asked.

"A brown cardboard falcon."

I reached into the box and plucked out Gandhi. "You mean, something like *this*?"

Turning the paper bird over, we both read *Paige Turner* written on its back in an even hand.

"Wow," breathed Natalie. "Is that . . . ?"

"Yep," I said. "The stuff dreams are made of."

The brown cardboard figure lay in my palm. Such a slight slip of paper, the cause of so much mischief.

As I gazed at it, visions of ice-cream mountains and fudge lakes began to form in my head.

"Chet, you're going to give that to Paige, aren't you?" asked Natalie.

I smiled dreamily.

"Uh, Chet? Chet?"

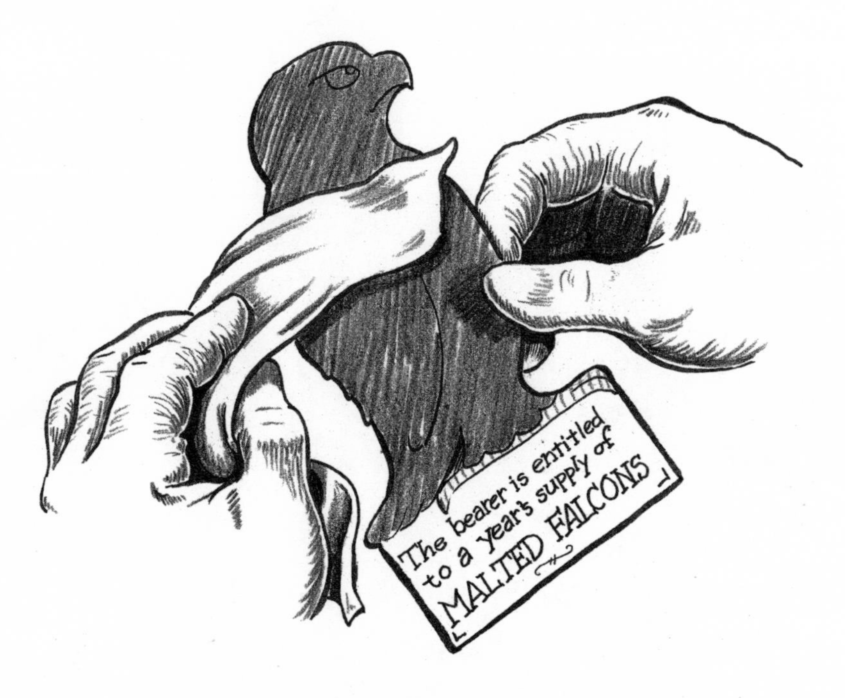

Chet gets catty
with the press in
Trouble Is My Beeswax

The kitten stretched and leaned on the railing beside me. "I hear Old Man Ratnose made you guys take that test over. Twice."

"Yeah, so?"

I checked her out. The kitty's ginger-striped fur was fluffier than a cloud soufflé, and it shone like moonlight in a glass of milk. *She must spend a fortune on conditioner,* I thought.

"I hear it was because so many kids cheated."

"My, Grandma," I said, "what big ears you have."

"I've got twenty-twenty hearing, Mr. PI." Her ears swiveled. "See? No wax."

"And where'd you get your information?"

The kitten watched kids playing tag. "A little bird told me," she said.

Cassandra the Stool Pigeon, no doubt. That bird's mouth ran like a bully with a wedgie: fast and furious.

I turned toward the kitten and rested an elbow on the rail.

"Did you know that a couple of the sixth-grade teachers have also been having problems with cheaters?"

"No, but then I don't know the zip code for Kowloon, either," I said. "Why so many questions?"

The kitten straightened her whiskers. "It's my job to be nosy," she said.

"What, you're a principal?"

"No, silly, a journalist." She offered me her paw. "Kitten Caboodle, ace reporter for the Emerson Hicky *Daily Tattletale.*"

Great. Just what I needed—a reporter sticking her snoot into my business.

"Well, whoop-de-do and Kalamazoo," I said, ignoring her outstretched paw. "What's all this got to do with me?"

Her smile was as painted-on as a chocolate-milk mustache. "You're a detective," she purred. "And Emerson Hicky has a cheating ring. Tell me," she said, pulling out a notepad, "what progress have you made?"

I gritted my teeth. "None. I'm not on that case."

"Really?" she said. "That's not what I heard."

"Then maybe your hearing's only fifty-fifty."

She ignored me and scribbled on her pad.

"I can see the headline now," Kitten said. *"Cheating Ring Baffles Detective."*

I crossed my arms. "Look here, kitty cat. In the first case, I'm *not* investigating a cheating ring. In the second case, I'm not baffled. And in the third case . . ."

"Yes?"

"What does *baffled* mean, anyway?"

Look for more mysteries from the Tattered Casebook of Chet Gecko in hardcover and paperback

Case #1 *The Chameleon Wore Chartreuse*

Some cases start rough, some cases start easy. This one started with a dame. (That's what we private eyes call a girl.) She was cute and green and scaly. She looked like trouble and smelled like . . . grasshoppers.

Shirley Chameleon came to me when her little brother, Billy, turned up missing. (I suspect she also came to spread cooties, but that's another story.) She turned on the tears. She promised me some stinkbug pie. I said I'd find the brat.

But when his trail led to a certain stinky-breathed, bad-tempered, jumbo-sized Gila monster, I thought I'd bitten off more than I could chew. Worse, I had to chew fast: If I didn't find Billy in time, it would be bye-bye, stinkbug pie.

Case #2 *The Mystery of Mr. Nice*

How would you know if some criminal mastermind tried to impersonate your principal? My first clue: He was nice to me.

This fiend tried everything—flattery, friendship, food—but he still couldn't keep me off the case. Natalie and I followed a trail of clues as thin as the cheese on a cafeteria hamburger. And we found a ring of corruption that went from the janitor right up to Mr. Big.

In the nick of time, we rescued Principal Zero and busted up the PTA meeting, putting a stop to the evil genius. And what thanks did we get? Just the usual. A cold handshake and a warm soda.

But that's all in a day's work for a private eye.

Case #3 *Farewell, My Lunchbag*

If danger is my business, then dinner is my passion. I'll take any case if the pay is right. And what pay could be better than Mothloaf Surprise?

At least that's what I thought. But in this particular case I bit off more than I could chew.

Cafeteria lady Mrs. Bagoong hired me to track down whoever was stealing her food supplies. The long, slimy trail led too close to my own backyard for comfort.

And much, much too close to my old archenemy, Jimmy "King" Cobra. Without the help of Natalie Attired and our school janitor, Maureen DeBree, I would've been gecko sushi.

Case #4 *The Big Nap*

My grades were lower than a salamander's slippers, and my bank account was trying to crawl under a duck's belly. So why did I take a case that didn't pay anything?

Put it this way: Would *you* stand by and watch some

evil power turn *your* classmates into hypnotized zombies? (If that wasn't just what normally happened to them in math class, I mean.)

My investigations revealed a plot meaner than a roomful of rhinos with diaper rash.

Someone at Emerson Hicky was using a sinister video game to put more and more students into la-la-land. And it was up to me to stop it, pronto—before that someone caught up with me, and I found myself taking the Big Nap.

Case #5 ***The Hamster of the Baskervilles***

Elementary school is a wild place. But this was ridiculous.

Someone—or some*thing*—was tearing up Emerson Hicky. Classrooms were trashed. Walls were gnawed. Mysterious tunnels riddled the playground like worm chunks in a pan of earthworm lasagna.

But nobody could spot the culprit, let alone catch him.

I don't believe in the supernatural. My idea of voodoo is my mom's cockroach-ripple ice cream.

Then, a teacher reported seeing a monster on full-moon night, and I got the call.

At the end of a twisted trail of clues, I had to answer the burning question: Was it a vicious, supernatural were-hamster on the loose, or just another science-fair project gone wrong?

Case #6 ***This Gum for Hire***

Never thought I'd see the day when one of my worst enemies would hire me for a case. Herman the Gila Monster was a sixth-grade hoodlum with a first-rate left hook. He told me someone was disappearing the football team, and he had to put a stop to it. *Big whoop.*

He told me he was being blamed for the kidnappings, and he had to clear his name. *Boo hoo.*

Then he said that I could either take the case and earn a nice reward, or have my face rearranged like a bargain-basement Picasso painted by a spastic chimp.

I took the case.

But before I could find the kidnapper, I had to go undercover. And that meant facing something that scared me worse than a chorus line of criminals in steel-toed boots: P.E. class.

Case #9 ***Give My Regrets to Broadway***

Some things you can't escape, however hard you try—like dentist appointments, visits with strange-smelling relatives, and being in the fourth-grade play. I had always left the acting to my smart-aleck pal, Natalie, but then one day it was my turn in the spotlight.

Stage fright? Me? You're talking about a gecko who has laughed at danger, chuckled at catastrophe, and sneezed at sinister plots.

I was terrified.

Not because of the acting, mind you. The script called for me to share a major lip-lock with Shirley Chameleon—Cootie Queen of the Universe!

And while I was trying to avoid that trap, a simple missing-persons case took a turn for the worse—right into the middle of my play. Would opening night spell curtains for my client? And more importantly, would someone invent a cure for cooties? But no matter—whatever happens, the sleuth must go on.